Only One You

by Linda Kranz

SCHOLASTIC INC.

ISBN 978-1-338-28777-6

30 22 23

Printed in the U.S.A. 40

First Scholastic printing, March 2018

Edited by Theresa Howell
Designed by Katie Jennings
Photography by Klaus Kranz

For Klaus—I give you my ♥ for safe keeping.

—L.K.

"It's time," Papa said.
"I think it is," Mama agreed.
"Time for what?" Adri asked.
Papa's voice softened,
"To share some wisdom."

Always be on the lookout

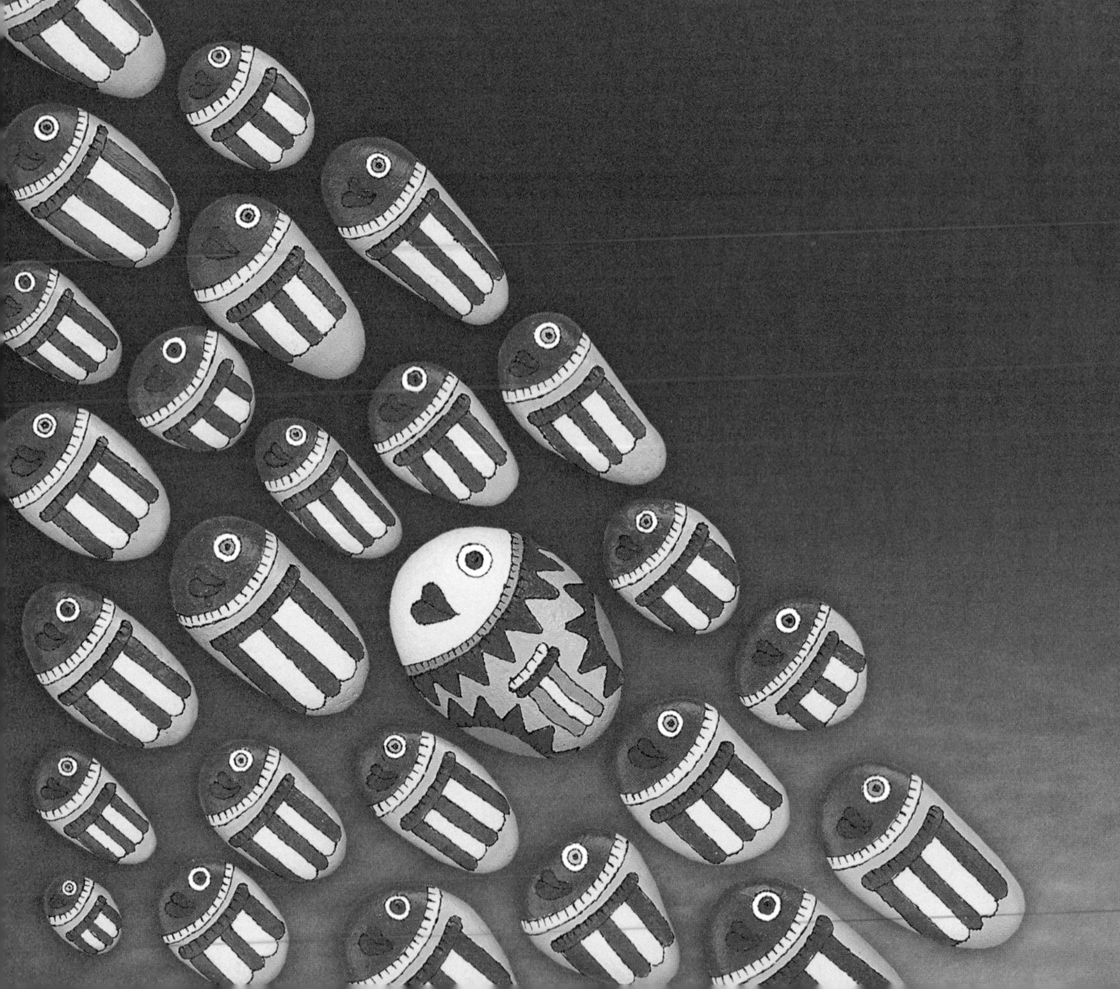

for a new friend.

Look for **beauty** wherever you are,
and keep the memory of it with you.

Blend in when you need to.

Stand out when you have the chance.

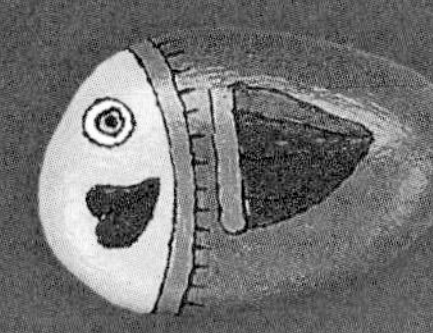

Find your own way.

You don't have to follow the crowd.

KNOW WHEN
to SPEAK;
KNOW WHEN to

No matter how you look at it,

there is so much to discover.

If you make a wrong turn,
circle back.

If something gets in your way,

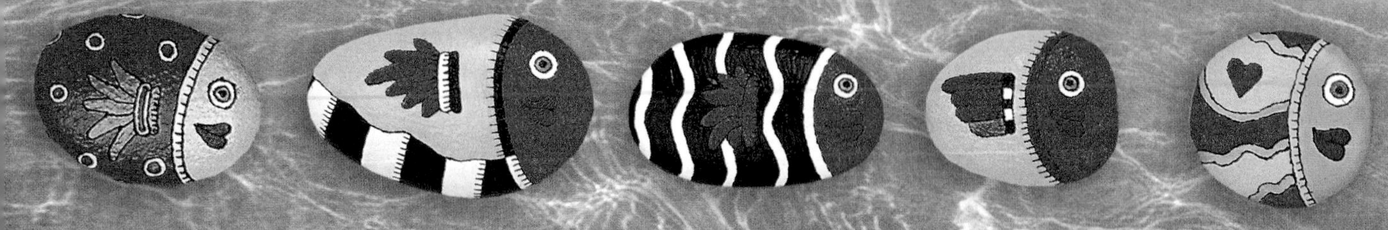

move around it.

set aside
some quiet time
to relax and

Every day.

art.

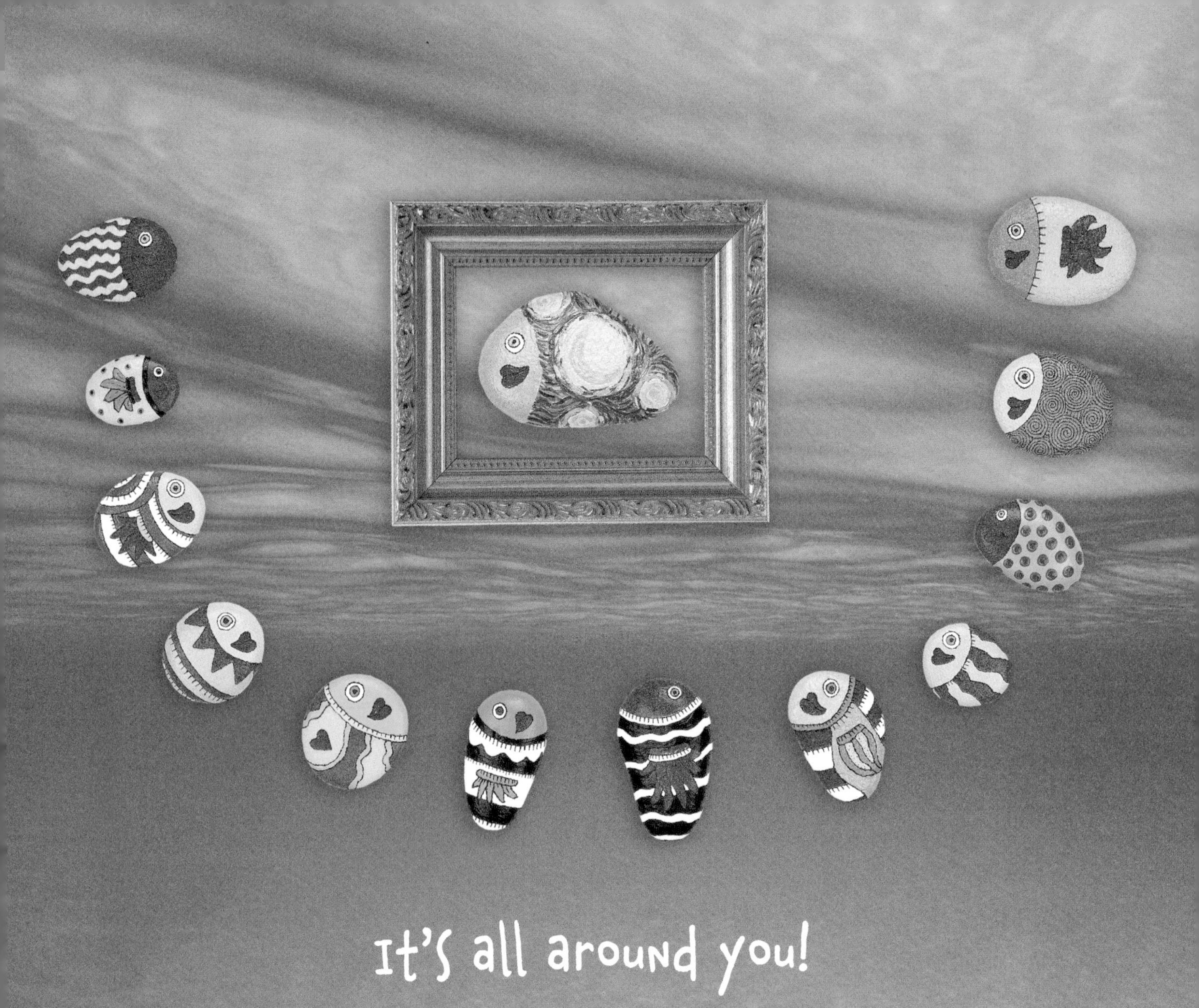

It's all around you!

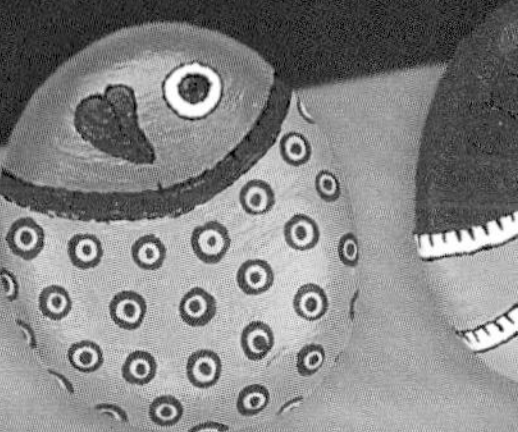

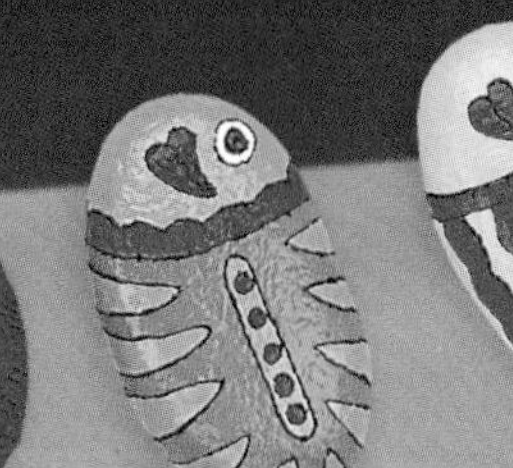

make wishes on the stars
in the nighttime sky.

"Thank you for listening," Mama said. "We hope you will remember."
Papa winked and whispered, "We know this is a lot for you to think about."
Adri did a backwards somersault and smiled.
He was excited to go out into the world with what he had just learned.
"Wait for me!" he shouted to his friends.

Before he swam away,
he turned back to his parents and said,
"I will remember."
Mama kissed Adri on the top of his head.
"There's only one you in this great big world," she said.

"make it a better place."